Tall Tales of Old India from a Very, Very, Very Long Time Ago

FOUR FORTUNE HUNTERS
The Panchatantra Book Five Retold

Narindar Uberoi Kelly

Illustrated by Meagan Jenigen

For My Granddaughter: Aurora Nathalie Ma Kelly

Order this book online at www.trafford.com
or email orders@trafford.com

Most Trafford titles are also available at major online book retailers.

Printed in the United States of America.

ISBN: 978-1-4907-4038-6 (sc)
978-1-4907-4041-6 (e)

Trafford rev. 07/10/2014

 www.trafford.com

North America & international
toll-free: 1 888 232 4444 (USA & Canada)
fax: 812 355 4082

Note To The Reader

I fell in love with these stories as a tween who stumbled across them in a library at a time when my family were refugees as a result of the partition of India between what is now Pakistan and India. I suppose part of the attraction of the stories was escape from the realities of being homeless in a part of India that seemed a different country, with people speaking different languages and eating food quite unlike anything I was used to. But the stories helped me by giving me some insight into what and why my parents were trying to teach me—and some appreciation for what I was resisting in a world turned upside down by our narrow escape from the violence and turmoil of our loss of home and country.

I decided I wanted my grandchildren to have access to these stories that meant so much to me, but in a language that they could easily understand. As I adapted the stories for modern readers, it occurred to me one of the great strengths of the Panchatantra (literally the five books) derives from what at first seems the sheer nonsense of listening in to animals talking like humans. Yet this absurd conceit of animals chatting and arguing and telling stories immediately establishes a strangely safe distance between the reader and these creatures. And even more strangely, we are transformed into observers and compatriots in their struggles with thorny issues of friendship, collaboration, conflict and ambition. If I was particularly taken with these tales at a time of vulnerability and uncertainty in my life, readers approaching and experiencing adolescence and young maturity (when *does* that process end?) are in some sense similarly adrift and puzzled by the strange new land of adulthood. Readers of these tales are assumed to be much like I was--expatriates operating in a new landscape they don't fully understand.

The genius of these stories is their relentless unwillingness to whitewash or romanticize adult life. They depict the ignoble as well as the noble, cruelty and deceit as well as honor, foolishness as much as cunning, deception as rampant as honesty. They show the underside as well as glimpses of fulfillment in adult life. The stories unveil the contradictory nature of adult life, its tensions, risks and dangers as well as its rewards. And it accomplishes this through the disorienting welter of stories within stories that pile up on each other to convey a kind of confusion that forms a powerful antidote to other literary forms designed to convey wisdom—like preaching, teaching, telling people what to do. Out of this confusion, somehow wisdom can escape as a form of deeper appreciation of the perils and tensions and value of leading a good life.

Narindar Uberoi Kelly

TALL TALES OF OLD INDIA

There was a king called Immortal-Power who lived in a fabulous city which had everything. He had three sons. They were truly ignorant. The King saw that they could not figure things out and did not want to learn. They hated school. So the King asked a very wise man to wake up their brains. The wise man, a Brahmin named Sharma, took the three Princes to his home. Every day he told them stories that taught the Princes lessons on how to live intelligently. To make sure they would never forget he made them learn the stories by heart. The fifth set of teaching tales Sharma told were:

Four Fortune Hunters

Sharma began

*"Never even think of actions
Ill-considered, consequential,
Disapproved, or done in haste.
Mind the tale of the Barber."*

"How come?" asked the three Princes, and Sharma told this story.

FOUR FORTUNE HUNTERS

The Panchatantra Book Five Retold

Narindar Uberoi Kelly

Illustrated by Meagan Jenigen

Four Fortune Hunters

Introduction

INTRODUCTION

The purpose of these stories has always been to teach basic knowledge and wisdom that makes for a better life. Each of the five 'books' in the original were organized around a theme: Loss of Friends, Making of Friends, War or Peace, Loss of Gains, Ill-considered Action.

Book Five here titled simply 'Four Fortune Hunters' is about misguided perceptions, drawing the wrong conclusions and coming to hasty and devastating judgment as a result of misreading another creature's situation. It is also about abject poverty, the bane of existence, and its consequences: the very worth of virtue, bravery, even learning, dims with poverty and people go to great lengths to escape it. But good or evil comes to good or bad people as Fate wills it and extravagant hope is an indulgence. One could say, the book celebrates the crucial role of common sense triumphing over pretentious learning, personal vanity and preposterous ambition. The greatest curse is that most dangerous ambition – greed.

After two initial *stand-alone* stories that highlight greed, the *frame* story becomes clear: it concerns four friends who decide to go abroad to alleviate their poverty and make their fortune. While a Master-Magician gives each of them a magic quill to help them on their quest, only well-considered action pays dividends and disregard of a friend's advice turns out to be a disaster for one of the fortune seekers. Chiding by Gold-Finder of his friend, Wheel-Bearer, (who ignored his advice and is now trapped in life-long suffering) and the Wheel-Bearer's defense of his action are illustrated through the *nesting* stories. These, mostly single stand-alone stories, are separated in this presentation from the main one by a simple conceit: the pages on the right of the open book contain the nesting stories. This allows parents reading aloud to young children, or adults themselves, to choose whether they want to read or ignore them. The frame story of the fortune hunting friends continues on the left hand pages with the text enclosed in a 'frame'. It can be read without interruption of the nesting stories. For the purists, the book can be read in its entirety left to right on the open pages to experience the original demanding design of this book of stories.

A word of caution: some of these stories illustrate Indian practices of many centuries past. Women are not often depicted or treated well, a phenomenon that continues to this day. But the stories have much to tell us. I trust that parents will help their children to understand the age-old realities described in this book and use the occasion to teach their own values.

Greedy Barber

There was an honest merchant who, as bad luck would have it, lost his fortune. He had lived his life in pursuit of happiness with both virtue and money but once reduced to poverty he suffered every humiliation until he could stand it no longer. He reflected *how good character, good conduct, good sense become worthless when poverty overwhelms a man.* In his despondency he resolved that life was not worth living so he would starve himself to death. That night, having made up his mind, he went to bed. He slept and dreamt that he saw a Monk made of gold coins and the Monk said to him "Do not lose hope. I am the gold earned by your ancestors. I will appear again in this form tomorrow morning. The minute you see me, you must club me on the head and my form will turn into pure gold."

The next morning, without having any breakfast, the Merchant wondered whether the dream of the Monk would come true. *After all, not all dreams come true. People who are sick or grieving or drunk or worried, all dream, but their dreams don't come true.* Meanwhile, the Merchant's wife had made an appointment for that morning with a Barber to come to the house to give her a manicure and her husband a shave. The Barber duly arrived and began to give the wife the manicure. Just then the Monk appeared and the Merchant did what he had been told to do in his dream the night before. He picked up a club and hit the Monk on the head. The Monk collapsed on the floor and turned into a pile of pure gold. The Merchant was astonished and delighted and hid the treasure in the middle of the house well out of sight.

However, the Barber had seen everything. When the Barber was leaving the Merchant gave him a big tip and asked him not to mention to anybody what he had seen. The Barber agreed but when he got home he thought that he could also become rich, in fact richer than the Merchant. He decided to club all the monks he could lure to his home. The Barber knew of a seminary nearby where young men went to study to become monks. So he plotted to lure all the young men who had already qualified to be monks to come to his house under the false impression that he was a pious man and needed their help. He told the monks that he had some valuable manuscripts that needed to be copied and that he would pay them well. The young monks often earned money for the seminary by acting as scribes to the outside world, so many agreed to come to the Barber's house. Some were genuinely eager to help the Barber as well as their seminary, some were just greedy to earn good money when their order of monks did not usually allow them to do so.

When they arrived at the Barber's house, he clubbed each of them on the head. Some died but some were just badly wounded. None turned into gold. The cries of the wounded were heard by neighbors and other villagers and soon soldiers arrived to arrest the Barber and take him to court. When questioned about his crimes by the Judge, the Barber wanted to know why the Merchant had not been arrested also. The Judge heard the Barber explain what had happened at the Merchant's house and sent for him. The honest Merchant described what had happened to him. The Judge ordered the Barber be impaled for he had heedlessly killed many monks and injured others. *"No person"* the Judge said *"should take action without properly seeing, understanding, hearing or examining the matter at hand. Only well-considered action should ever be undertaken.* Otherwise, like the lady and the mongoose, remorse will follow you all your life." "How is that?" asked the Merchant, and the Judge told this story.

THE LOYAL MONGOOSE

A Brahmin and his wife lived in a small town with their toddler son and a pet Mongoose the wife had reared as if it were her second son. She fed the Mongoose like her son, giving him breast milk and good baby-food and baths. But she didn't really trust the Mongoose. She thought a Mongoose was a nasty kind of creature and might hurt her son.

One day, she said to her husband as she tucked her son in bed for a nap "Please be sure to protect the boy from the Mongoose. Do not leave him alone. I have to go to get some water from the village well." But the Brahmin husband did not pay any attention to his wife's request and left soon after to go beg some food for the family. He was not long gone when a big black snake came into the house and slithered into the baby's room. The Mongoose saw him and, being a natural enemy of snakes and fearing for the baby's life, fought with the snake and eventually killed him. Then, very pleased with himself, and with the snakes blood still all over his face, went off to meet the Wife on her way home.

But when the mother saw the Mongoose with blood on his mouth, she jumped to the conclusion that he had killed her son. So, without thinking, she hit the Mongoose on the head with her full water-jar and killed him instantly.

When she got home she saw her baby was safe and still sound asleep in his crib while the dead snake's badly mauled and bloody body lay nearby. She finally realized what had happened. Overwhelmed that she had killed the savior of her child she wept. When the Brahmin returned home she blamed him bitterly for not doing what she had told him to do and now their second son was dead. "You were greedy for food. You could have waited. Remember the greedy fellow who had a whirling wheel on his head?" "How was that?" asked the Brahmin, and his wife told him this story.

Four Fortune Hunters

There were four fast friends, all Brahmin men, all very poor, who decided to get together to discuss their common plight. *They all knew that poverty was the bane of existence. Charm, courage, wit and good looks are useless without money in playing the social game. Friends, relatives, even children keep their distance; the worth of virtue, bravery and even learning dims with poverty.* So the friends decided to try and make money no matter the cost. It was better to be dead than penniless. They figured *there are six ways of making money: begging, serving the upper classes, working on a farm, teaching school, trading or becoming money lenders.* Only trading seemed to have no downside, allowed making big money, and therefore was most acceptable to them. However, even trade that leads to profit can have seven temptations or related challenges: use false weights and balances, price gouging, opening a pawn shop, somehow attracting repeat customers, selling livestock or luxuries, and foreign trade. Again, they found problems with each and eventually decided upon foreign trade and therefore foreign travel.

After they had been travelling a while, they met a Master-Magician and went with him to his monastery. He asked them where they were from, where they were going and why. The friends replied "We are pilgrims seeking powers of magic ourselves. We are very poor and have decided to search for riches or die. They say that great effort pays off. Do, please, show us a way of making money, no matter what we have to do to get it." So the Master-Magician made four magic quills and gave one to each of the four friends saying "Wherever the quill drops, the owner will find treasure." The first quill dropped and the owner found the soil was covering a hoard of copper. He told his friends "We can share. You can each take all you want" but the others did not see the value in doing so. In fact they encouraged him to leave his find and go on with them but he declined. He took his copper and turned back and the three other friends continued their search. Further along, the second quill dropped and the owner found a trove of silver. He was delighted and told his friends. "We can share. You can each take all you want" but the others were sure there would be gold ahead and urged him to continue along with them. But he declined, took his silver and turned back.

The third quill dropped and the owner found a cache of pure gold. He was thrilled and said to his friend "We can share. You can take all the gold you want" but the other said "You are foolish. We will find gems next so come ahead with me." But Gold-Finder declined. "I will wait here for you. You are being greedy and should not go off alone." But the fourth friend went on. He travelled a long time, became very confused and was very hungry and thirsty. He finally saw a human being on a whirling platform with a whirling wheel on his head. The Wheel-Bearer was clearly in pain and drops of blood dripped down his face. The last friend said "Why are you standing there with a whirling wheel on your head? Anyway, tell me where I can find water. I am dying of thirst." The minute the last friend said this, the wheel left the other man's head and settled on his head! "What is this? This wheel hurts. When will it go away?" The other man replied "When someone who holds a magic quill like yours and speaks as you just did, only then will the wheel leave you." The friend asked "How long were you here?" "Centuries!" came the answer "The wheel is the result of a curse by the Master-Magician to keep greedy people from reaching or taking the last treasures which belong to him." And he vanished. Eventually, the Gold-Finder friend came looking for the last friend. He heard his sad tale and scolded "You didn't listen to me. Remember the scholars without common sense who made a lion and died." How was that?" asked the poor Wheel-Bearer, and the Gold-Finder told this story.

A Dead Lion Lives Again

There were four Brahmins who were close friends. They had grown up in the same village. Three were true scholars and had achieved high honors for their knowledge of all the arts and sciences. The fourth had, however, taken a different road. He was a simple man of sense, good common sense, and had refused to follow in his friends footsteps. One day the friends were chatting and one of them said "What is the worth of all this learning we have acquired? We should travel, win the patronage of Kings and get rich." So they left their village for foreign lands.

They had not gone far when one of them said "We won't *all* win acclaim. One of us has no scholarship at all. So he will not be sharing our wealth. Maybe he should turn back?" The second friend agreed but the third friend said "No. This is no way to behave towards our childhood friend. Please do come with us and share any wealth we acquire." So the four friends continued their quest.

When they were passing through a jungle, they came upon the bones of a dead lion. One scholar said "Hey, why don't we test our knowledge on this dead creature? I can set all the bones together to make a proper skeleton." The second scholar rushed to say "I know how to get together flesh, blood and skin." "Well, I know how to give it life" said the third scholar. So the first and second scholars set about and performed their tasks successfully. But, as the third scholar was about to breathe life into the dead lion, the fourth friend, the sensible one, stopped him, and said "Don't do it. If you bring a lion to life, he will kill all of us." The third scholar replied "You really are a fool. I am not going to do something that will destroy our scholarship!" The man of sense responded "O.K. If you are going ahead, please wait a minute while I climb up that tall tree." When the third scholar breathed life into the lion, he killed and ate all three scholars and then wandered off to find some water. The man of sense climbed down carefully and returned home.

The Wheel-Bearer, however, objected to the story. He said "But not all men of great sense do well. Sometimes those with very little sense can, with a little bit of luck, do very well. Remember the proverb Hundred-Wit was on the head, Thousand-Wit hung from the shoulder, but I, Single-Wit am alive in clean clear water?" "How was that?" asked the Gold-Finder, and the Wheel-Bearer told this story.

Hundred-Wit, Thousand-Wit, Single-Wit

Two fish who were very smart lived together in a large pond. They were nick-named Hundred-Wit and Thousand-Wit because they were very brainy. They made friends with a frog who was considered simple whose nick-name was Single-Wit. Despite their differences, the three friends often had good conversations together hanging out at the edge of the pond.

One day they overheard some fishermen who were standing at the water's edge surveying the pond. "Look" said one, "this pond is teeming with fish. Let us come here early tomorrow morning with our rods and nets and get a good catch."

The three friends were obviously upset. The frog was the first to speak. "What should we do? Stay or flee?" Thousand-Wit laughed and said "I don't think the fishermen will show up but even if they do, I can outsmart them. So I shall stay." Hundred-Wit added he agreed with his fish friend. "Why should we leave home? *The wise always find a way out of problems.*" But the Frog said "I am Single-Wit and I am telling myself to flee." So, later that night, the Frog and his wife fled to another body of water nearby.

Late next morning what did they see but two fishermen going home with their catch of the day. "See" said the Frog to his wife "One carries Hundred-Wit on his head, the other hangs Thousand-Wit on his shoulder but I, Single-Wit am alive with you in clear clean water."

The Gold-Finder heard the Wheel-Bearer's story but continued "Yet, *one should not always disregard a friend's advice.* I told you to stop and share my gold. You were too proud of your smarts and too greedy. You should have remembered the singing donkey." "How Come?" asked the Wheel-Bearer and the Gold-Finder told this story.

Singing Donkey

There was a donkey named Headstrong who made friends with a Jackal. The Donkey worked for his master who was a laundryman but at night he was allowed to roam free. The Jackal and Donkey would raid different fields at night, eat their fill, and went to their own homes early before dawn and before the watchful farmers were up.

One night, the Donkey, standing in a cucumber field, said to his fellow thief, the Jackal "The night is so beautiful. I feel like singing." The Jackal was astonished and advised the Donkey "Please don't sing. We are thieves. Singing will alert the farmers and you will come to grief." "You really are not a music lover. Haven't you heard the magic of music?" the Donkey responded. "I have" said the Jackal but your braying is harsh and will carry across the fields. Why do something that can only harm you?" "So you think I cannot sing" said the obstinate Donkey. "I am conversant with musicology and have an educated taste. How can you stop me?" "OK" said the Jackal "Sing your heart out. I will stay at the edge of the field as a look out for the farmers."

The Donkey began to sing and the farmers came running. They beat him and put a millstone round his neck when he was unconscious and went home. When he awoke the Donkey ran away. The Jackal said to himself with a smile. "You sang so well and now you have a medal for it round your neck!"

*

Gold-Finder again reminded the Wheel-Bearer "You should have listened to me." "Yes, you are right" said the Wheel-Bearer finally. "*Without wit, one should at least listen to a friend.* I should have remembered the simple weaver who came to a fatal end." "How was that?" asked the Gold-Finder, and the Wheel-Bearer told this story.

Simple Weaver

A Weaver lived with his wife in a small town in the east of the country. He worked hard and made a modest living. One day, as bad luck would have it, all the pegs in his loom broke. So he took his axe and went into the nearby forest to look for a suitable tree to cut down and use the wood to make new pegs.

After spending a considerable time searching for just the right tree, the Weaver came upon one which would provide him plenty of new weaving pegs and tools. So he lifted his axe to cut it down. Just then he heard a voice say "Please spare my tree. I have lived here happily for a very long time." "But", replied the Weaver "I have no choice. I am so sorry to do this. However this is the right tree from which to make my pegs and without them my family will starve. Couldn't you please move to another tree?" The voice above, which belonged to a tree fairy, then said "You are a good man. I will grant you one wish for anything you like if you do not cut down my tree." The Weaver was very pleased and replied that he needed to consult with his friend and his wife before choosing the wish, so he would return the next day.

On his way back to town, he met with his friend, explained what he needed and asked for advice on what wish he should ask the fairy. His friend said promptly "Ask for a Kingdom. Then you can be King and I can be your Prime Minister and we can live happily ever after." "That sounds like a very good idea but I need to check it out with my wife." "Oh don't do that" said his friend. *"Wives should be loved and showered with gifts but one should never seek their advice."* "You may be right" said the Weaver but I will consult her. She is a good wife."

The Weaver then went home and told his wife what had happened, what the fairy had offered and what his friend had advised. "Oh, your friend is a barber!" she explained, "what sense does a barber have? Being a King and having to rule brings not only trouble but also danger of being overthrown. Don't listen to your friend." Then what should I ask for?" asked the Weaver. To which the wife replied "You make a good but modest living. Why not ask the fairy to double it by giving you an extra pair of hands and a second head? That should make us comfortable".

So the simple Weaver went to the fairy and asked for a second pair of hands and a second head which she readily gave him. On the way, the townspeople saw him, thought he was some kind of demon, were frightened, and killed him.

*

"Yes" said the Wheel-Bearer "*any man becomes ridiculous when seduced by absurd dreams. That is why they say "don't indulge in extravagant hope* or you will become all white like the father of Moonson." "How was that?" asked the Gold-Finder, and the Wheel-Bearer told this story.

Day Dreaming Brahmin

There lived a poor Brahmin who made his living by begging. Once he was given a good amount of barley-meal. After eating some, he saved the rest in an earthen pot and hung it above his bed. As he was about to fall asleep, he started to day dream:

There would be a famine and his store of barley-meal would fetch one hundred rupees. With that money he would buy a pair of goats who would breed every six months and within a couple of years he would have a herd which he could sell. Then he would buy a pair of cows who would have many calves. These he would sell to buy buffaloes. Eventually he would buy and breed horses that would sell for gold. With the gold he would buy a great mansion and then a rich man would offer his daughter to him and she would bring a large dowry.

"Then we will have a son whom I will name Moonson. When my son is old enough he will want to sit on my knee as often as possible. But I will be busy and sometimes I will ask my wife to take him and if she doesn't do it right away, I will have to kick her behind."

As the Brahmin was day dreaming of the kick, he actually let fly a high kick that shattered the barley-meal pot above his bed and made him white from head to toe.

*

"You are right" said the Gold-Finder "greedy people do not pay attention to the consequences of their deeds, just think of King Star." "What happened to King Star?" asked the Wheel-Bearer, and the Gold-Finder told this story.

Avenging Chief-Monkey

There was a small city-state ruled by a King named Star. He was very indulgent and kept a pack of monkeys for his son's amusement. There was also a herd of rams. The Prince enjoyed getting the rams to fight each other and have the monkeys do all kinds of tricks. He had his servants feed the animals well. But the rams were aggressive and went into the royal kitchens quite often to get whatever was available for food. The cooks were very unhappy and fought the rams off as best they could to keep the palace dinners from been spoiled.

The Chief-Monkey saw the recurring problems between the cooks and the rams. He worried that there would be a fight and the cooks would one day hit the rams with a burning log and set fire to some of the rams. If the burning rams went into the stables next door, the hay there would light and the horses would get injured. If that happened the monkeys would be in trouble because the veterinarians believed that the only way to heal a horse that has been burned is by using monkey fat for balm. That would lead to the killing of monkeys.

The Chief-Monkey was known for his foresight and knew the situation was a tragedy waiting to happen. So he went to his troop of monkeys, explained what he feared, and suggested they leave and go to the woods for safety. One should flee senseless quarrels. But the young monkeys didn't want to give up their easy life. They simply ignored the Chief-Monkey's warning as undue worrying by an old-timer. So the Chief-Monkey left alone for the woods. He could not bear to hang around and witness the destruction of his troop that he thought was inevitable.

A day later the Chief-Monkey's fears materialized. The rams came in to the kitchen, the angry cook threw a burning log, two rams' coats caught on fire, the rams ran to the stables, set the store of hay ablaze and the King's horses were badly burned. The King did not think through the consequences of his actions and ordered the whole troop of monkeys be killed so the animal doctors would have the monkey fat he needed to heal the King's horses.

As it happened, the Chief-Monkey had come to the edge of a pond when he left the palace, and was about to enter it to quench his great thirst, when he noticed that there were many footprints going to the pond but none coming back. So he decided to be cautious and drank the water standing on the shore using the hollow stem of the lotus flower as a straw. Now there was a Monster who lived in the pond and ate every creature that entered the deep water. He had noticed the Chief-Monkey's caution and said to him "Well done. Your caution has helped you escape from me. I eat everyone who jumps into the pond for whatever reason. I have taken a liking to you. Is there anything I can do for you?"

23

By this time the Chief-Monkey had heard the news of the slaughter of his clan. He could not let it go and was set on revenge. So he immediately asked the pond Monster "If I lured people to enter your pond, how many can you eat?" "As many as you bring me and more!" replied the Monster. "I live in deadly hatred of King Star" explained the Chief-Monkey. "I will try and awaken his greed by a plausible story but to be successful I need you to lend me your necklace of rubies." The Monster understood the Chief-Monkey's plan and decided to befriend him by loaning him his ruby necklace.

The Chief-Monkey returned to the palace wearing the ruby necklace and told King Star a false story about how he acquired it. The King and his people all wanted to go to the pond so they could get similar necklaces and become rich. When the Chief-Monkey saw they were all hooked, he led a procession to the pond but insisted that he and the King be last ones to jump in the pond. Thus all the King's subjects jumped into the pond and all were eaten by the Monster. Then the Chief-Monkey climbed up a high tree pretending to be a lookout and from his safe position shouted down to the King "You killed my entire clan and now I have killed all your subjects. I didn't kill you because you are my king but I see no wrong in repaying evil with evil."

*

Having told the story, Gold-Finder asked the Wheel-Bearer "Please bid me Goodbye. I want to go home." "But you can't leave me in this plight! Deserting a friend will lead you straight to hell," replied the Wheel-Bearer. "That is true" said the Gold-Finder "but only if I can really help and the friend is in a salvageable situation. The more I look at you the more I am reminded that if I don't leave right now I will also be caught in Twilight's cruel grip." "What are you saying?" asked the Wheel-Bearer, and Gold-finder told this story.

A Credulous Demon

Once there lived a King who had a very beautiful daughter named Pearl. She lived with her parents in the palace and had a magic circle around her to prevent her from being kidnapped. However, there was a Demon who pestered her every night and the poor Princess Pearl felt extreme fear and trembled and tossed and turned feverishly. She couldn't get rid of the unseen Demon and he couldn't take her away because of the magic circle.

One night, the Demon showed himself to the Princess and she, at once, pointed him out to her maid saying "Look there is the Demon who comes with Twilight to torment me. Is there any way to keep him away?" The Demon misunderstood her words. He thought I am not the only demon who visits. There is another called Twilight, who also comes every night but also cannot carry her off. I had better take the form of a horse and find out what form the other demon takes and what power he has. So the Demon turned himself into a horse and stood in the King's stables on the lookout for his rival.

As it happened, a horse thief came into the stables and chose the Demon-horse to steal. He saddled him and put the bit in his mouth and kicked him with his spurs. The Demon-horse now worried that the horse-thief was his rival and took off at a brisk pace. When the horse-thief struck him with a whip the Demon-horse galloped away at a pace the horse-thief had never before experienced. When the rider tried to control the Demon-horse, it galloped even faster. Realizing that something was very wrong, the horse-thief steered the horse under a banyan tree and jumped up and caught a branch while the Demon-horse kept running on. Once separated, they were both relieved. But then a monkey interfered and called out to the Demon-horse "Why run from an imaginary danger? Your rider is just a man. Kill him." So the Demon changed back into his usual form and came back to the banyan tree. But the thief who was sitting in the branch below the monkey grabbed the monkey's tail and starting biting and chewing it very hard. The monkey felt trapped and dared not move or say anything. The Demon looked at him and said "To judge by your face, dear monkey, you have been caught in Twilight's cruel grip" and the Demon fled.

*

Once the story came to an end, Gold-Finder said again "Bid me farewell. I want to go home. You may stay here and suffer the consequences of your greed and disregard of a friend's advice." "That is not so" said the Wheel-Bearer "Good or evil comes to good or bad people as fate wills it. As the old tale goes, whether a hunchback, a blind man, or a princess with three breasts, fortune favors whom it wills." "How so?" asked the Gold-Finder, and the Wheel-Bearer told this story.

Three Breasted Princess

In a city in the center of the North country, lived a King whose Queen gave birth to a three-breasted girl. As soon as he heard the news, the King summoned the Chamberlain and ordered that the girl be taken from the palace and left in the forest so that no one would ever know the sad facts. The Chamberlain answered that the King should consult holy Brahmins, ask their opinion, so that any action he undertook under the sad circumstances would not offend any laws, human or divine. "For the proverb says a prudent man always enquires into things beyond his understanding like the Brahmin caught by a fiend but let go again." "How was that?" asked the King, and his Chamberlain told this story.

The Inquiring Brahmin

In a forest there lived a cruel fiend who treated everyone who wandered into his territory very badly. One day a Brahmin was crossing the forest. The Fiend caught him, climbed on to the Brahmin's shoulders, and made him carry him wherever he wanted to go in the forest. Since the Fiend was sitting on the Brahmin's shoulders with his legs dangling in front, the Brahmin noticed that he had soft supple feet with no corns or calluses. So the Brahmin asked the Fiend "Please Sir, why are your feet so tender?" and the Fiend replied "I am under a vow never to touch the ground with my bare feet."

Soon they came to a pond where the Fiend wanted a wash so he told the Brahmin to stand at the edge of the pond and not stir until the he had bathed. The Brahmin realized that if he waited, the Fiend would eat him but if he ran away, the Fiend would probably not come after him immediately because of his vow. So the Brahmin escaped.

After listening to the story, the King consulted with the Palace Brahmins and inquired from them what he should do. They advised that the King should not look upon his daughter and that he should make a proclamation that if any man would marry the Princess with three breasts, he would give the man a hundred thousand pieces of gold and the couple would have to live in a foreign land.

Time passed and no one offered for the hand of the Princess until she was of marriageable age. Then a young man, who was blind, lived in a nearby city and had a hunchback servant to help him manage daily chores, remembered the proclamation and decided to offer to marry the Princess. Shortly thereafter the Blind Man married the three-breasted Princess and with the Hunchback, the threesome left for foreign lands with their riches.

They found a comfortable house and lived together for some months in harmony. But the Hunchback did all the work while the Blind Man dozed on a cot all day. After some more time passed, the three-breasted Princess and the Hunchback became very close and started an affair. One day, the Princess asked the Hunchback to find her some poison so she could kill her husband and marry him. The Hunchback found the body of a deadly snake that the Princess cut up and seasoned to make a delicious smelling stew. As it was simmering on the stove, the Princess asked her husband to stir it periodically for she had to go shopping and the Hunchback was busy in the fields. The husband readily stood up and began his task in the kitchen. As the steam from the poison stew rose and stung his eyes, the Blind Man suddenly noticed that he could see some light. After a while, his vision cleared completely and he could see! He was no longer completely blind! Then he looked in the pot to see what could have caused the miracle and saw the deadly snake pieces in the bottom of the pot and realized what was going on. There was a plot to kill him. But he kept his cool and when the Princess wife and the Hunchback returned he did not let on that he could see and watched them very closely. He tried to figure out the chief culprit. But when the Hunchback kissed the Princess, the husband lost his cool. He picked the Hunchback up by his feet and literally hurled him at the Princess. The result was totally unexpected: the blow shoved the Princess' third breast back into her body and the hunched back of the lover straightened as he legs were pulled hard!

*

When the Wheel-Bearer finished the story, the Gold-Finder said "You are right. Good things can happen but only if fate wills it. I hope things work out for you. Goodbye." And the Gold-Finder left.

"The End" announced Sharma. "You mean you are not going to tell us any more stories?" asked the three Princes. "That is correct" said Sharma. "From now on, you will be on your own."

Remember

Should you choose
To learn as taught
You will never lose
No matter what.

ACKNOWLEDGEMENTS

As I have noted elsewhere, the *Panchatantra* stories (literally Five Books) have been part of India's oral and scholarly tradition for at least two thousand years or more. They have been told and retold all over the world and have influenced many literary genres, particularly those containing animal characters and 'nesting stories' i.e. one story in another story in another story. Sometime towards the end of the twelfth century, the seminal version of the *Panchatantra* was written by Vishnusharma in Sanskrit and has formed the best known rendition ever since. It is comprised of a vast array of folk wisdom interspersed with eighty-five stories which collectively serve as a guide book of sorts on how to live a wise and good life. Many translations of the text are available in English and some selected stories have been published for young children. However, the entire collection has never been adapted for casual readers, whether teenagers or adults.

My goal is to make the core of the *Panchatantra* easily accessible to the English speaking world. I have delved deeply into three authoritative, literal, translations of the complete text of the *Panchatantra* from the original Sanskrit by three eminent scholars: Arthur W. Rider (1925), Chandra Rajan (1993) and Patrick Olivelle (1997). Their work represents the best of what serious academics have to offer. I am clearly indebted to them. Nevertheless, the original in its entirety remains rather difficult to register and enjoy for non-academics. I have used their translations to understand and stay as close to the original of the *Panchatantra* as possible. Beyond that, the way I have organized the five books for a lay audience, the telling of the stories, the language used, and the summary of the wisdom highlighted by the stories, are entirely mine.

I have read and re-read the stories in various forms over the last fifty years. I wish I had a way of publicly thanking all the authors I have read on the subject of the *Panchatantra*. Suffice it to say, their work taught me that these ancient stories are the essence of Indian wisdom and values that deserve a wide international audience.

Throughout this venture, my husband Michael has been my strongest backer, my sharpest critic, my meticulous editor, and my most longsuffering love. I cannot thank him enough. I also owe thanks to my children, Kieran and Sean, who never failed to point out that my stories were not PC enough for children, and to my friends, Roland, Judy and Jon, who did not hesitate to point out that my story-telling was too confusing even for adults. I hope they will see that I took their judgments seriously.

I hope that my enthusiasm for these stories is catching. Cheers.

Narindar Uberoi Kelly, June 2014

MORE TALL TALES OF OLD INDIA

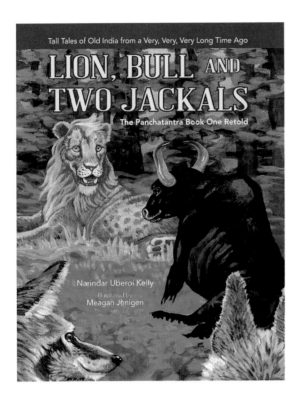

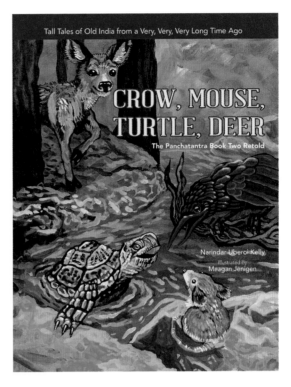

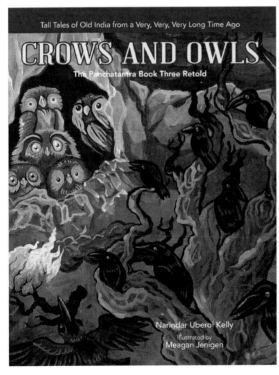

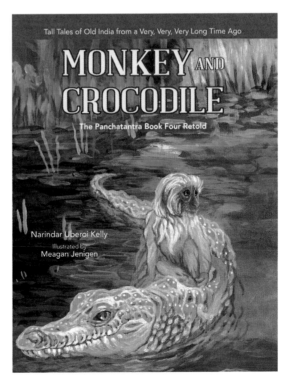

The Panchatantra Retold
Narindar Uberoi Kelly
Illustrated by Meagan Jenigen

CPSIA information can be obtained
at www.ICGtesting.com
Printed in the USA
BVXC01n1632210714
359734BV00001B/3